This book belongs to

Thinking Big

Published by Advance Publishers
www.advance-publishers.com

Written by Victoria Saxon and Annie Auerbach
Illustrated by Jeffrey Oh and Andrew Phillipson
Editorial development and management by Bumpy Slide Books
Illustrations produced by Disney Publishing Creative Development
Cover design by Deborah Boone

ISBN: 1-57973-019-1

"Ouch!" said Dot. "Stop pinching my antennae, you big meanies!"

Dot meant it, too. Those ant boys had been teasing her all day, and she was sick of it.

Well, she would show them. Someday she would have wings. Then the boys would be sorry. They would wish they could fly, too.

Dot chased the boys down one of the tunnels in the anthill. They ran around a corner. Dot followed, but she couldn't find them.

Then she saw a glimmer of light coming through a hole in the tunnel. The boys had dug all the way through the ceiling to the outside!

Dot raced toward the hole. "You're gonna get in big trouble!" she shouted after them. "You're not allowed to make holes in the ceiling!"

Dot scrambled up through the hole and popped outside.

The boys ran fast, but Dot knew she had to catch up to them. Struggling, Dot stretched her wings. Maybe they weren't grown in yet, but she could at least try using them.

She began flapping her wings as hard as she could. Then she leaped into the air. She was flying!

Suddenly Dot hit the ground with a crash! Well, maybe she had just been jumping.

"Dot!" someone said sternly. It was her mother, the Queen. "What did I tell you about playing rough?"

"That I shouldn't do it until my wings grow in," Dot mumbled.

"That's right," the Queen replied. "Just be patient. It will happen any day now."

Just then Dot's big sister, Atta, came over. Atta was in training to be queen, and she was always bossing Dot around. "Dot," said Atta, "you should—"

"Excuse me," Dot interrupted. "You're not the queen *yet*, Atta."

Suddenly a big grain stalk fell down. It landed right on Atta! All the other ants were worried. Luckily, Atta wasn't hurt.

"Sorry!" called Flik. He was wearing his new grain-picking invention. "I'm so sorry, Atta. I didn't see you there."

"Flik, please put down your silly invention and just get to work," Atta said sternly.

Dot ran after Flik. “Hey, wait up!” she cried.

“Oh. Hello, Princess,” Flik said. He was always nice to Dot. He made her feel like a grown-up ant.

“I like your inventions,” Dot told him.

She wanted to cheer up her friend. Dot knew Flik worked hard trying to invent things to help the colony.

"Well, you're the only one who does," Flik replied, smiling weakly. "I'm beginning to think nothing I do works."

"I know what you mean," said Dot. "I keep trying to fly, but it's not working either. My mother says it's because I'm too little."

“Being little’s not such a bad thing,” Flik told her.
Then he picked up a rock. “Here,” he said to Dot.
“Pretend this is a seed.”

Dot looked at the rock. It wasn't a seed. It was a rock. Flik sure could be silly sometimes.

"Just *pretend* it's a seed," Flik urged. "Everything that made that giant tree over there is already contained inside this tiny little seed. All it needs is some time and a little bit of sunshine and rain!"

Dot was confused. “This rock will be a tree?”

“No, no,” Flik said. “Remember, we’re only *pretending* it’s a seed. Then the seed will become a tree. It’s like you.”

Dot giggled. She hoped she would never be a tree!

"What I'm trying to say is, you just have to give yourself some time to grow," Flik explained. "You're still a seed."

"I get it!" declared Dot, smiling.

Dot sure was glad Flik was around to help her understand things. But a few months later, Flik got into trouble again. This time Atta told him to leave the colony and never return.

Dot was sad. She would miss Flik a lot.

Shortly after Flik left, the mean grasshoppers came to the colony. Every season, they made the ants pick grain for them.

This time the grasshoppers were really angry because the ants had not collected enough food. Dot and the Blueberries were frightened. They ran to hide in their clubhouse.

While she was hiding, Dot overheard one of the grasshoppers say that they were going to squish the Queen!

"I've got to do something!" Dot cried. "I'll find Flik! He'll help me!"

Before the other Blueberries could stop her, Dot dashed out of her hiding place and started running.

Immediately the grasshoppers spotted Dot and started to chase her. She ran through the grass until she came to a cliff. But when Dot tried to leap out of the way of the grasshoppers, she fell right over the edge!

Dot closed her eyes and began pumping her wings as hard as she could. Suddenly she wasn't falling anymore. When Dot opened her eyes, she couldn't believe it! She was flying!

Dot flew and flew, looking for Flik. She searched through forests and along dried riverbeds. Finally, after a whole day of searching, she spotted him.

"Flik! Stop!" she cried as she flew down to him.

"Dot!" Flik gasped. "What are you doing here?"

"You have to come back and help," Dot said. "I heard the grasshoppers say that they were gonna squish my mom!"

Flik bowed his head sadly. “I can’t help,” he said.

Dot couldn’t believe what she was hearing. “Please, Flik!” she begged.

“I can’t do anything right,” sighed Flik. “I’d just make things worse. After all, my invention almost squished Atta.”

Dot remembered the story Flik had told her about the little rock growing into the big tree. Flik had used that story to cheer her up. Well, if it had worked for her, then it should work for Flik, too.

Dot found a rock and handed it to Flik. "Pretend it's a seed, okay?" she said.

Slowly, a grin spread across Flik's face. Dot was getting more grown-up every day.

Together, the two ants headed back home.

When they got there, Flik managed to outsmart the grasshoppers and rescue the entire colony—including the Queen. And it was all thanks to his little friend Dot, who dared to think big.

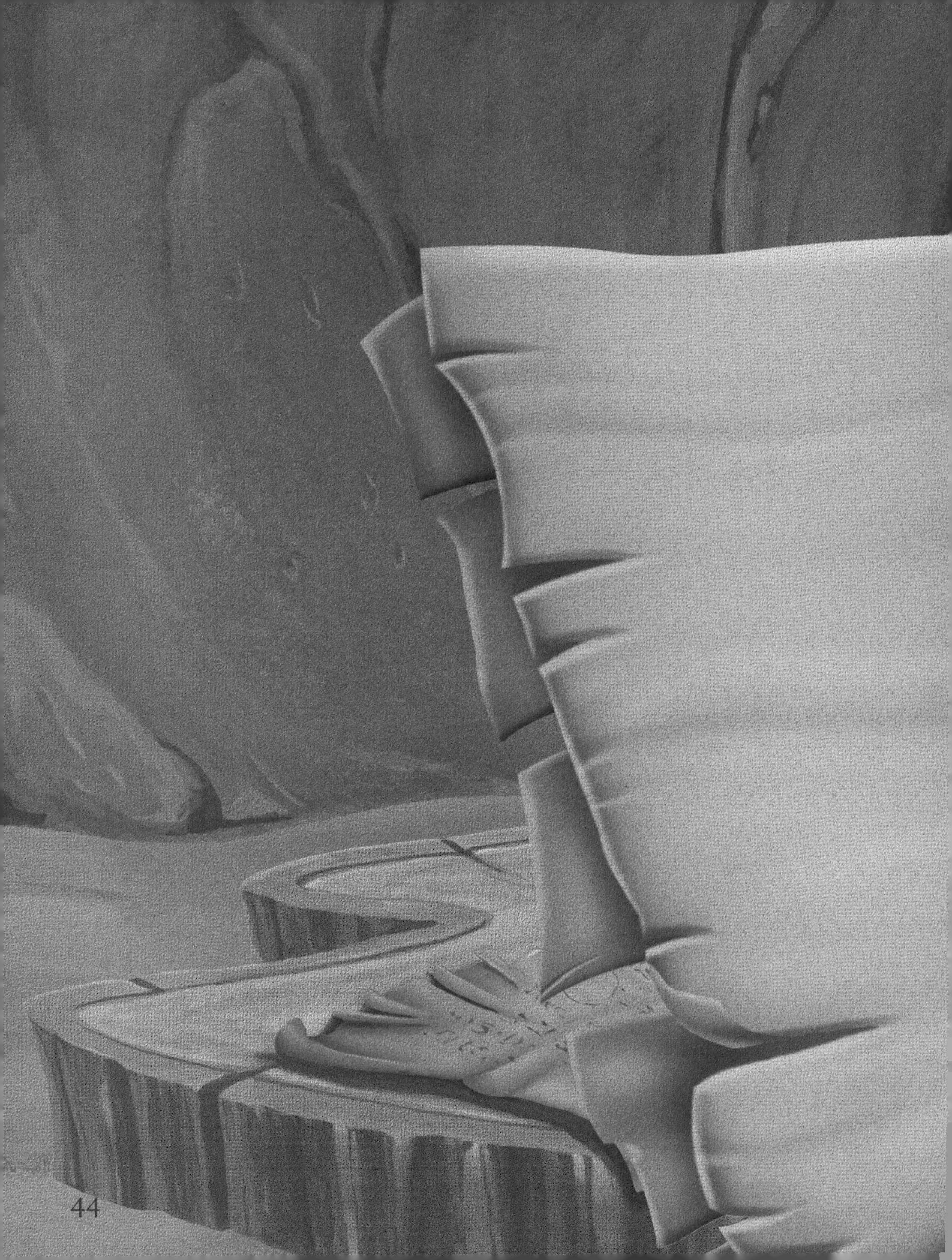

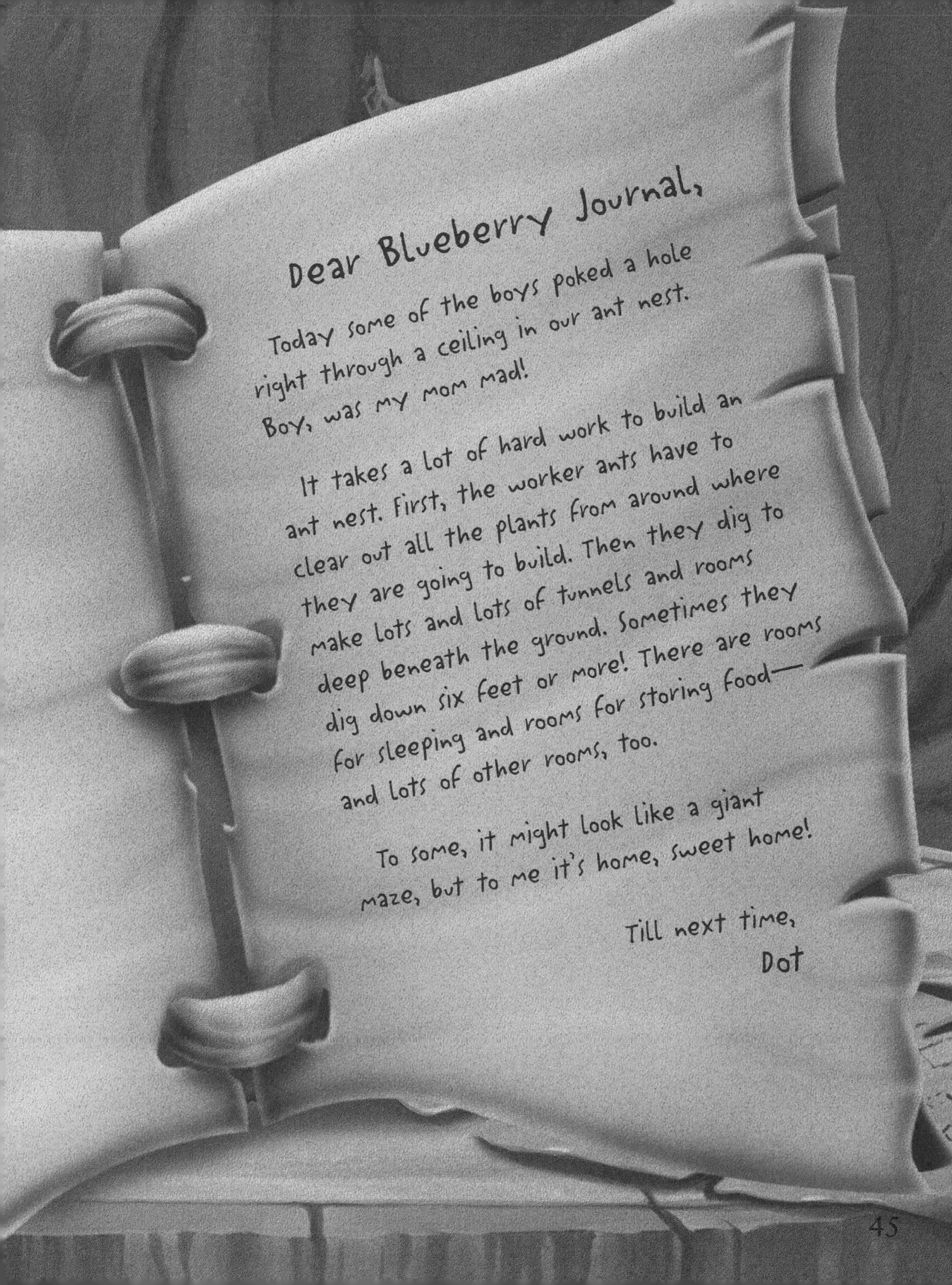

Dear Blueberry Journal,

Today some of the boys poked a hole right through a ceiling in our ant nest. Boy, was my mom mad!

It takes a lot of hard work to build an ant nest. First, the worker ants have to clear out all the plants from around where they are going to build. Then they dig to make lots and lots of tunnels and rooms deep beneath the ground. Sometimes they dig down six feet or more! There are rooms for sleeping and rooms for storing food—and lots of other rooms, too.

To some, it might look like a giant maze, but to me it's home, sweet home!

Till next time,
Dot